Sabrina
The Teenage Witch™

Magic
Handbook

Sabrina
The Teenage Witch™
Magic
Handbook

Patricia Barnes-Svarney

AN ARCHWAY PAPERBACK
Published by POCKET BOOKS
New York London Toronto Sydney Tokyo Singapore

To Lynda DeLuca, teacher, good friend . . . who always helps me discover life's everyday magic.

Special thanks to editor extraordinaire Lisa Clancy and Elizabeth Shiflett.

Special thanks to the people who made this book possible: Gina Centrello, Donna O'Neill, Lisa Feuer, Julie Blattberg, Karen Clark, Gina DiMarco, Nancy Pines, Patricia MacDonald, Twisne Fan, Agnes Birnbaum, Paul Ruditis, Diane Hobbing, and the staff of Pocket Books, Archie Comics, and Viacom Productions.

AN ARCHWAY PAPERBACK Original

An Archway Paperback published by
POCKET BOOKS, a division of Simon & Schuster Inc.
1230 Avenue of the Americas, New York, NY 10020

ISBN: 0-671-02427-2

First Archway Paperback printing December 1998

10 9 8 7 6 5 4 3

Printed in the U.S.A.
IL 5+

Cover design by Lisa Litwack

Book design and composition by Diane Hobbing of Snap-Haus Graphics

Contents

Introduction

Hi! I'm Sabrina.

You probably think of magic whenever you see me and my aunts, Zelda and Hilda Spellman. We're all witches. (Well, I'm half mortal, half witch.) And we all use our powers to create magic. Oh, except Salem. He's our black cat who's really a warlock who tried to conquer the world. But that's another story for another book.

You probably also know that I'm learning to fly around on my magic vacuum cleaner. And that I've been known to accidentally scatter truth sprinkles around school.

But did you also know that all of us—you *and* me—are surrounded by magic every day? Just look around you. I'll bet there are mysteries lurking in your kitchen that you never thought about, like why does my bread have all those tiny holes in it? Why do some smells smell better than other smells?

(If I could, I'd show you some everyday magic by

borrowing my aunt Zelda's top-of-the-line lab-top chemistry set, but she's overly protective of it.) So I'm going to show you some of the magical things that surround you every day. All right, without a magical chemistry lab we won't be able to conjure up a black hole in the kitchen sink, but I can tell you things about the color black you never knew.

We'll smell, push, or pluck some things, and we'll just stare (and wonder) at other things. (A scientist would say we're *observing*.) Oh, and although *I* have to keep my magic a secret from my friends, you *can* show your friends the everyday magic you've learned here. So let's get going!

—Sabrina

One last note before we start:

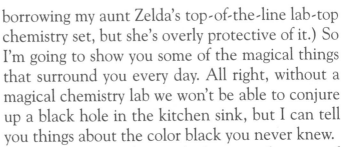 Some of the activities—such as cutting, cooking, or lighting a candle—may require adult supervision. Don't forget to double-check with a parent or an adult before starting any of these experiments.

Now We're Cooking

My aunts Zelda and Hilda love to cook up a good recipe, and so do I. But I'll bet the witch recipes we cook in the Spellman house don't look quite like what you cook up in your kitchen.

I once made magic jumping beans. Yeah, I admit it. I cut corners on the recipe. But how was I supposed to know that a giant beanstalk would grow in the backyard once I tossed the beans out? No one tells me anything.

Let's find out what magical things you can cook up in your kitchen. First, some hints: Stay away from the Magic Hair Soup; it will make your hair grow much too long and too fast. And don't bother making the Crystal Ball Stew; the words get caught in your teeth.

But here are some everyday magical things you can try:

Get the Umbrella!

If you're in the mood to cook up a storm…

Then again, don't cook up a storm. Been there, done that. It gets everything wet in the kitchen. And Salem and my aunts really hate eating under an umbrella indoors.

Don't worry. I have a suggestion. There is a magical way to make it rain in the kitchen, and you don't have to get wet. All you need is some fresh warm tap water, a quart jar with a lid, and some ice cubes. It's that easy.

Pour just enough warm water to cover the bottom of the jar. Then set the lid upside down over the mouth of the jar. Place three or four ice cubes in the upside-down jar lid. Wait about ten minutes and then check the underside of the lid. You'll notice it's raining inside of the jar!

4

This is sort of what happens when it rains outside. Follow me here; I read this in my science book when I was in Mr. Pool's class: Some of the water in the bottom of the jar evaporates, changing into a gas called water vapor. The water vapor then changes back into a liquid when it condenses on the cold, ice-filled lid. More drops form, and the drops turn to drips.

Clouds do the same thing. They're really made up water vapor. When clouds rise into the colder upper air, the vapor condenses into water droplets, join other droplets, and eventually form larger drops of rain.

At this point, I would probably use my powers to add a bit of lightning and thunder—but only on those days when I wasn't going on a picnic with my boyfriend Harvey Kinkle.

What Did You Say...er...Write?

I admit it. I sometimes write notes to my friends, like Harvey or Val, and pass them in between classes. One time I wrote a note at home, and I didn't want Salem to know what I'd written. When he looked over my shoulder, the paper was blank. He was completely baffled. After all, I was writing with lemon juice! (Just thinking about it makes my mouth pucker.)

Here's how you can write magic invisible notes to your friends. You'll need a shallow dish, enough lemon juice (from real lemons works best) to cover the bottom of the dish, paper (the type of paper you use at school is fine), a lamp with a 60- or 75-watt bulb, and a small paintbrush. Pour the lemon juice into the dish. Dunk the paintbrush into the juice, then write a special message on the paper. Let the writing dry, then pass the note to your friend.

Your friend will be surprised—it's a blank piece of paper! Tell your friend to hold the paper close to the lightbulb (but don't let the paper touch the bulb). The secret message will soon appear. And you don't have to stick to lemon juice; you can use onion juice or vinegar instead.

What really happened?
The part of the paper that absorbed the lemon juice (or onion juice or vinegar) burns, or oxidizes, more easily than the rest of the paper when you hold it near heat. What you're seeing when the message appears is really a chemical reaction.

Yeasty Beasties

My friend Valerie and I went to the mall the other day and watched a woman making bread at the bakery. She stuffed some really gooey bread dough into a pan, then shoved the pan into the oven. By the time we were shopped out and walked by the bakery again, the bread was done—and twice the size that it had been before it was baked.

Now this is magical to me: the bread rises because of something called yeast. As strange as it may seem, the little yeasty beasties are actually from the fungus family, and they are considered *living organisms*. It's nothing to get grossed out about—it's natural.

Because yeasts just love sugar, they eat their way into the heart of the bread. The funny bubbles we see in bread are from a gas called carbon dioxide that the yeast gives off as it eats the sugar. But because the raw dough is so gummy, the gas can't escape. The dough rises, and the heat of the oven "cooks in" the bubbles. In fact, bakers have known

about yeast for almost four thousand years now, not only for bread making but in making certain drinks as well. The yeast ferments the liquids, turning the sugar into alcohol and carbon dioxide.

Now let's get magical.

You'll need:
2 small bowls
1 cup flour
2 teaspoons sugar
14 teaspoons lukewarm water
1 teaspoon dry yeast

Put 7 teaspoons of lukewarm (not hot—that will kill the yeast) water into each bowl. Add the 1 teaspoon of yeast *to one bowl only*, stirring until the water becomes milky. Now add ½ cup of the flour and 1 teaspoon of the sugar *to each bowl,* and stir with a fork until it is mixed and you have made two dough balls. Let the dough stand for 15 minutes in a *warm* spot. Which one seems to get bigger in a shorter period of time? It seems like magic, but it's merely the reaction of the yeasty beasties.

Float Your Eggs

I tend to float above my bed when I sleep. In my case, my witch powers help me stay afloat in the air. But there is something you can do that seems just as magical: you can make an egg float!

 First, make a magic solution: Gather 2 two-cup measuring cups, some salt, and 2 fresh eggs (you'll be able to use them again if you don't break them). Pour 1 cup of fresh tap water into each measuring cup. To one of the cups, add 5 tablespoons of the salt and stir. Now gently drop an egg into each measuring cup. The egg in the fresh water will sink; the egg in the salt water will float, just like I float above my bed. If you want to make this trick look even more magical, slowly add some more fresh water to the salt water so that the egg looks as if it's suspended in the middle of the measuring cup.

W h a t really happened? The salt increases the density of the water so that it holds up the less dense egg. That's why people who swim in the Great Salt Lake in Utah tend to float and can't really sink. I guess Salem wouldn't need his Greeny the Turtle swimming tube to swim in the Great Salt Lake!

Busting Out All Over

If you just mention certain words, I can smell them: pizza, garlic, onions, lemons, popcorn.

Popcorn?

Yeah, you know the smell of the popcorn when you walk into a movie theater? It's almost as if it's calling to me. (Then again, maybe it's my friends calling me, telling me to buy the popcorn already so we can sit down and watch the movie.)

 You can also do a really cool trick with popcorn. I learned this from my friend Valerie. You'll need a mug or a cup, some popcorn kernels, a metal cookie sheet, and some water. Now fill the mug or cup with the popcorn kernels and add as much water as possible. Set the cup on the cookie sheet and then put it under a bed, on a counter, or anyplace where you want to surprise someone—or yourself! This will take five or six hours, but then you'll hear some mysterious noises.

The reason for these noises is that just as popcorn reacts to the heat of a stove by popping, it also reacts to water by "waking up" as the kernels swell from the water.

I'm sure glad it doesn't take *me* five or six hours to wake up!

13

It's Pepper! Achoo!

I love pepper. And although I use it on my salad and in my soup, pepper really doesn't like me. It makes me sneeze, and that can be disastrous if I'm in the middle of casting a spell!

 I'm not the only one who runs from pepper. To prove this, you'll need some black pepper, a bowl containing 2 quarts of cool, fresh tap water, a saucer, some liquid detergent, and a toothpick. Sprinkle the pepper over the surface of the water in the bowl. Put a few drops of the detergent in the saucer and then dunk one end of the toothpick into the detergent. Put the detergent end of the toothpick into the pepper water—and watch the pepper run toward the sides of the bowl.

Right. It's just like the time I had that huge wart on my face and all my friends seemed to run the other way!

What's happening here? The water molecules pull equally on all the pepper flakes. When you add the detergent, the water molecules and the detergent get together, weakening the pull of the water molecules. The pepper scrams as a result.

15

Pushing and Pulling

Sometimes I feel as if I'm being pulled in all directions. I have to go to school, hang with my friends, do my chores, and try to study for school *and* for my witch's license. Oh, and don't forget Harvey stuff, football games, and phone calls. What's a girl to do?

Little did I know that toothpicks could get pushed and pulled, too. My *Magic Handbook* has a great section on this. Let's see…"perfect pets, prickly porcupines"…Here it is, "push and pulls." All you need is a bowl, some fresh tap water, a sugar cube, a small bar of soap, and two toothpicks. Fill the bowl with water; then float the two toothpicks in the water, about one-half inch apart. Touch the sugar cube to the surface of the water between the two toothpicks. Then take the bar of soap and touch the water again between the two toothpicks.

Did you notice the difference? The toothpicks seemed to be pulled *toward* the sugar cube but are repelled by the soap.

There's a simple explanation: The sugar cubes have plenty of holes in them, and when the water flows into the holes, it sets up a tiny current in the water, pulling the toothpicks toward the sugar. The soap pushes them apart by weakening the water molecules at the surface. Sounds like magic to me.

Goop and Me

I remember one day when I really felt as if everything was going wrong. My aunt Hilda told me there was one way to feel better—make a gigantic wiggly-jiggly flan, her happy dessert. And it really was good, if a bit hard to fit into your average oven.

Don't tell Aunt Hilda, but I've made something that's even more fun because it's gooey and gummier. Sabrina's Goop, I call it. Original, huh?

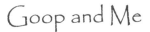 Here's what you do, but you'll need some adult supervision: Gather together some light corn syrup, two packets of unflavored gelatin, and about a half cup of water. Boil a quarter cup of the water and add the two packets of gelatin. Take the mixture off the heat and stir, letting the gelatin soften as you stir. Then add about a quarter cup of corn syrup, still stirring. As the mixture cools, continue to add water to keep it thick and sticky. In fact, the goop should look really stringy.

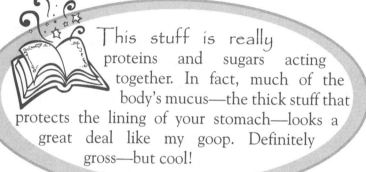

This stuff is really proteins and sugars acting together. In fact, much of the body's mucus—the thick stuff that protects the lining of your stomach—looks a great deal like my goop. Definitely gross—but cool!

19

OK, so you can't eat this stuff, but now you have a bowl of goop. What can you do with it?

You can use it in a haunted house on Halloween, or to scare people anytime. Add weird things like raisins, buttons, and spaghetti, let it sit in the fridge for a few hours and *poof!* Instant grossness. Turn out the lights and ask someone to stick their hand in the bowl. Don't tell them it's just proteins and sugars. Do tell them it's a lot like the lining of your stomach. Mmmm. . . .

Shake, but Don't Bake

Want to do something so magical that it happens faster than I can point? Just get an unopened plastic—*do not use glass*—bottle of seltzer, and stand it upright in the freezer overnight. When you open the freezer door the next morning, the seltzer inside the bottle will *still be* a liquid. Now carefully take the bottle out of the freezer and give it a quick shake. In a flash, all of the liquid will turn to ice!

This is the type of experiment that even scientists aren't sure about. What *probably* happens is the seltzer gets supercooled but stays a liquid. Then either the bubbles in the bottle or a particle on the side of the bottle hits the supercooled seltzer. The ice forms around the bubbles or particle, and starts an ice-chain reaction.

Some Body

Because I'm a half-witch, strange things can happen to my body—like the time I caught the finger flu, and every spell I cast turned into a disaster. Or spellfluenza, when I kept sneezing, sending my witch powers to anyone around me. (Once, that person happened to be Libby, the girl who keeps trying to make my life miserable. Yikes! What a mess!)

In spite of the strange things that happen to me, my body actually seems magical—and probably yours does, too. Certain smells, for instance, change my mood, making me feel calm or ready to roll. Certain colors make me feel happy, and others make me want to exercise. There are even herbs that freshen my breath, which is great for parties.

Smells That Tell

I can always tell when my aunt Zelda has taken a wrong turn in her quantum lab-top chemistry lab—the smell around the house is enough to make Salem's fur stand on end. But when Valerie and I go out shopping, one of our favorite stores sells scented candles and soaps, and some of those smells make me feel great!

In fact, there's even a science that uses smells to release certain chemicals in our bodies and make us feel great; it's called aromatherapy. Most of the smells come from concentrated oils of aromatic plants, called essential oils. But it takes quite a few plants to get an oil. For example, it takes about 250 pounds of roses to make 1 ounce of rose essential oil. (Hmmm…I wonder what they do with all those thorns?)

It's easy to spread a great smell around the house. Sometimes I use candles. Other times I put a drop of essential oil into a dish of warm water,

then set it in a sunny window. As the water evaporates, the aroma fills the room.

Here are some of my favorite essential oils—and what I found out about them:

+Eucalyptus. Those cute koala bears in Australia love to eat eucalyptus leaves. For humans, the smell is very stimulating, and it's known to clear the mind. The oils are even used as an insect repellent.

+Lavender. Lavender has a soothing and refreshing scent, and its aroma helps you have a restful sleep. And lavender is great to smell if you're a little nervous. (It sounds like just the thing for those days when the Quizmaster tests me for my witch's license!)

* Remember! Use the oils only on the outside of your body—and only after you've asked a parent's permission!

✦Lemon. I bet you didn't know that the small yellow fruit in your refrigerator could be used in aromatherapy. But it is—and the citrus smell refreshes you and perks you up when you're feeling down.

✦Peppermint. You probably know what a mint tastes like. It almost feels cool when you bite into one—sort of like biting into a snowball! The smell is just as sensational and helps you stay alert and refreshed. Some people even place moistened peppermint leaves on their temples to get rid of a headache.

✦Rose. The smell of roses lifts your spirits—and I don't mean ghosts. If you're feeling a little sad, try  smelling a rose scent. It even helps you stay alert when you're studying. (I'll have to try it when I study for my next algebra test.)

Herbs Away!

Oils aren't the only things that can make the body feel good—so can herbs. No, this isn't Herb, an old boyfriend of my aunt Hilda's. These are herbs—the plants that humans have used for centuries for flavoring their cooking, for their healing quality in medicine, for their pleasant smell, and for growing in gardens.

You've probably seen herbs in the grocery stores, and you've probably tasted them in your food at home or at a restaurant, where oregano and basil are very common. Here's some information about some common herbs from one of my aunts' cookbooks:

✦**Rosemary.** Rosemary is used for cooking, but the evergreenlike branches are also great for smelling. Tell your parents that rosemary twigs on a barbecue give off a wonderful aroma; and if you have a wood-burning stove, they make the house smell great. (But don't ever throw anything on a

fire without checking with an adult first!) Rosemary oil can be used as an insect repellent, and if applied directly to the temples, it can often get rid of a headache.

+Parsley. You know that funny-looking little plant that sits on your plate in a fancy restaurant? That's usually parsley. Centuries ago people believed that only witches could grow parsley. Well, we know that's not true—parsley is one of the easiest plants for anyone to grow. It's used mostly for cooking. And if you eat that little parsley sprig on your plate, you'll find out that it's a great breath freshener—even if you've eaten garlic.

+Garlic. Speaking of which, did you know garlic was an herb? It's been around for centuries. In fact, the Roman soldiers were given the herb daily to keep their strength up. (I hope they had plenty of parsley to chew on, too!) Garlic is used in many foods, and scientists believe that it's great for the heart and the digestive system.

Sleepy-time Help

I admit that my sleep habits are probably a bit different from yours and your friends'. As I've said before, I tend to float about four feet above my bed. But there are some nights when I can't seem to get to sleep. So I do something that seems pretty magical to me: I drink some milk before I go to sleep, and it really helps. But why?

The reason is pretty neat. According to brain scientists, milk contains a chemical called tryptophan. The tryptophan allows the body to release chemicals called melatonin and seratonin. Melatonin is necessary for sleep, and seratonin helps to calm us down. Not everyone can drink milk, but those who can, often use milk to help them sleep.

When the Eyes Don't Have It

Neat picture, right? It's of a ghost and a haunted house. As a witch, I can certainly say that not all ghosts live in such houses. Sometimes they live in haunted garages.

 This is "eye magic," so be sure to try it yourself before you show it to your friends. Stare at the ghost while you count out about ten seconds. Then look quickly over to just under the archway. What do you see?

When I tried this on Salem, he said he saw a gateway and a haunted house in the background—but then, what does he know? He's a cat, not a human. What you should see is the outline of the ghost on the white field under the gateway.

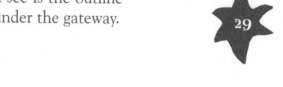

The outline of the ghost made an impression on the back of your eye. Then when you looked at a white background, you "saw" the ghost. There are very tiny cells at the back of your eye that gather light and turnit into something our brains can understand.

Get the Paint Out

Did you ever wonder where the expression, "I'm so blue," came from? Me, too, until I realized that colors really can affect us. Colors cause our moods to change, speed up our heart rate, and make our brains work harder. My science teacher told me that even the rooms inside the International Space Station—the space station that will soon orbit above the earth—will be painted certain colors to help the astronauts' moods during their long stay in space.

How do most colors affect us? Blue is used for relaxation, but it's also used in gyms to help you get a better workout. Red gives us energy and keeps us alert. Pink calms us down. Yellow helps us to think better. Orange is uplifting, making us happier. And green helps us keep a balanced mood.

Hey, I wonder what mood I'd be in if I pointed a finger and—*poof!*—my bedroom walls turned into *all* those funky colors at once?

Who Said I Was Hot?

Because of my powers, I have an infinite wardrobe. So I can dress myself in almost any outfit I desire in a split second. (Not that my aunts always like what I wear—but that's another story.)

What I do know about clothes is how dark and light clothes can sure make a difference. I went to a football game once to watch Harvey play (okay, okay, so he was warming the bench, but, hey, I was there to support him), and I wore a white sweater. It was chilly that day, even though the sun was shining. Valerie was sitting next to me, and she wore a dark blue sweater. She wondered why I was shivering—it seemed warm enough to her.

I realized later that there was a kind of magic going on here: the light sweater I was wearing *reflected* the light from the sun, but her dark sweater *absorbed* the light (and heat) from the sun, warming Val up. Although I won't be wearing my black witch's robe to the next football game, I may be wearing my dark sweater if it's cold enough.

Sweat It Out

According to my aunt Vesta, I don't sweat—I *perspire*. Either way, I know I sweat when I walk fast, when I have to take a final exam, and especially when the Quizmaster asks me questions for my witch's license!

Where does sweat come from? In school we learned that sweat . . . er . . . I mean perspiration comes from sweat glands located in certain spots all over our bodies. When we get hot, either from exercise or nervousness, these glands release a liquid in the form of sweat. This is the body's way of cooling us down. You know how you feel cool before you towel off after a shower or bath? The water is evaporating and cooling you down. Sweat acts in the same way: the sweat evaporates and causes our bodies to cool down.

Cool! Really!

Do Geese Have Bumps?

Goose bumps should really be called people bumps. After all, who's ever seen a goose with bumps? All I want to know is do geese have human bumps? Go figure.

I remember one time, before I learned I was a witch, I accidentally got locked out of the house. I had to sit on the porch in the cold until Aunt Hilda came home from a recital. I can still see the goose bumps popping up all over my legs and arms. They made my skin look like the plucked skin of a chicken. Not at all what I'd call fashion model material.

Of course, it's body magic again. Goose bumps, gooseflesh, or, more appropriately, human bumps appear when humans are cold or scared. Tiny muscles attached to the hair follicles on the skin cause our hair to stand on end. When a person is cold or scared, the muscles contract (sort of squeeze together), and little bumps appear around the hair. We call them goose bumps.

My Magic Handbook says that the greatest number of goose bumps per person per square mile occurs on Halloween. Cool.

35

Head of Ice

If you're like me, you probably crave something cold to drink during the hotter times of the year. In the summertime my aunts, Salem, and I wander over to the ice-cream store. Aunt Hilda orders a pistachio ice-cream cone, Aunt Zelda dips into a fruit sorbet, and Salem gets plain vanilla in a cup, with those cute little colored sprinkles, of course.

Me? I sometimes get a chocolate cone—and a brain freeze!

You probably know the feeling. It's as if someone bopped you over the head, making your sinuses (the passages or cavities in your skull, but particularly around your nose) and your eyes feel as if you just took a fast trip to the planet Pluto.

Brain freeze is usually called an ice-cream headache. My aunt Hilda told me what scientists think really is happening: When the icy stuff hits the back of your palate in your mouth, it activates a nerve center that controls the blood flowing to your head. When the cold hits, the nerves cause the

blood vessels in your head to swell. And—*Bam!*—you have brain freeze. Luckily it usually lasts for less than a minute.

How can you avoid freezing your brain? Try keeping cold foods at the sides of your mouth, not just in the middle touching the palate all the time. Or if you feel a headache coming on, wait a bit and let your tongue warm up your palate before you dig in again. (But watch out for Salem. He will try to convince you that *he* should eat your ice cream so *you* won't get brain freeze!)

Noise Makers

What about those times when everyone is taking a test in class, and suddenly, without warning—*achoo!*—I sneeze? And what about the times when I eat my lunch too fast and end up with the hiccups? People always stare at me. Sometimes it's worse than having a witch wart on my forehead.

I have to keep telling myself that these are just more magical reactions of our bodies. Sneezing is the body's way of reacting to something that irritates the nose, whether it's dust or something else that you sniffed. When you sneeze, you take in a deep breath first. Then the sneeze comes out at speeds that can reach more than 100 miles per hour. That's faster than my flying vacuum can go! (Coughing is sneezing's slowpoke cousin; its greatest speed is only 60 miles per hour.)

And what about hic . . . hic . . . hiccups? Hiccups are really spasms of the diaphragm, the muscle below the stomach area that controls how much air we can put into our lungs. They are usually caused

by too-rapid eating, very hot foods, or stress.

Methods of getting rid of the hiccups are a matter of personal choice. They range from eating a spoonful of sugar to holding your breath for a short time. Some methods work, some don't; it varies from person to person.

Salem says petting him gets rid of hiccups, too. Hmmm . . .

Making Magic

My aunts are always trying to help me with my magic, but sometimes I just need to practice, practice, practice. After all, I didn't learn that I was a witch until I was sixteen, and it takes time to learn to spell.

I do know there are some magic tricks you can do with numbers and cards. I found some in one of my magic books, but not all of them. So Salem—even though he is intolerable sometimes—taught me a few of the card and number tricks he's learned over the centuries. And even though I know the trick behind the cards or numbers, some of them still seem like magic to me.

Don't Be Square

Numbers seem magical to me. They allow us to add up the money we need to buy something at the mall. They tell us how much flour to add to cake batter. And they let me know when it's time for Harvey to take me out on a date. (I don't want to miss *that!*)

But there is more to numbers—a way of looking at them called Magic Squares. According to Salem, these squares were invented by the Chinese centuries ago, and he should know—he's been around for a long time. They're known as "Order 3" squares because there are three rows and three columns. Since the numbers, when added or multiplied in certain ways, equal the number in the center of the square, they seem magical. In fact, the first square, called the *lo-shu* by the Chinese, seems so magical that people sometimes wear it as a lucky charm.

4 9 2
3 5 7
8 1 6

1st square

7 12 5
6 8 10
11 4 9

2nd square

16 36 8
12 20 28
32 4 24

3rd square

4²

For the first square, when you add the numbers across the rows or down the columns or diagonally, the answer is always 15—or 3 times the center number. To get the numbers in the second square, we added 3 to every number in the first square. Now when you add all the numbers in the second square across the rows or down the columns or diagonally, the answer is now always 24—also three times the center number. Finally, we multiplied each number in the first square by 4 to get the numbers for the third square. Now when you add all the numbers in the third square across the rows or down the columns or diagonally, the answer is always 60—again, three times the center number.

Sometimes Salem shows me some cool things. (Notice the word "sometimes.")

43

How Old Are You?

Speaking of Salem, I'm not even going to guess how old he is—or how old my aunts are. My aunt Hilda probably went to school with Galileo Galilei. Wow! Imagine the conversations *they* must have had.

Speaking of age, did you know there's a magical way to figure out your friend's age? It has to do with the magic of numbers again, especially the number 9. To me, it's just a number, but according to Salem, over the centuries, the number 9 was thought to have mysterious properties.

Here's how you guess someone's age: First, have your friend write her age on a slip of paper without letting you see it. Ask her if she is over or equal to 10 years old, or less than 10 years old—without telling you her age. Then tell your friend to write your lucky number (90) below her age. Tell your friend to add the two numbers together. Now tell your friend to cross out the first digit in the total; then tell her to take the crossed-out number and add

it to the total if she is equal to or older than 10 years old, and subtract it from the total if she is younger than 10 years old. Then ask your friend what that total number is—and add your magic number to the total—9. The result is your friend's age. Voilà!
Equal or older than 10 years old:

Examples:

```
 12 (her secret age)                              12
+90 (your secret number)                         +90
 102 ──► Cross out the first digit ──► 02
              add 1                               +1
                                                   3
              add 9                                9
                                                  12
```

Younger than 10 years old:

```
  8 (her secret age)                               8
+90 (your secret number)                         +90
 98 ──► Cross out the first digit ──► 8
           subtract 9                             -9
                                                  -1
              add 9                                9
                                                   8
```

Tricky Kings

Sometimes my friends and I get together to play cards. You know, games like Fish or Crazy Eights. After my friends left one day, Salem said he'd teach me a few things about cards—in other words, card tricks.

There was one trick he picked up from a king who lived during the Middle Ages, and it's one you can do, too. And not only do you get to do a trick, but you can be a storyteller, too.

 First, remove all the kings from the deck, arrange them in the shape of a fan, and show them to your friends. What you *also* do is hide four other cards behind the kings so that your friends can't see the extra cards.

Next comes the story: "Once upon a time, four kings lived in huge castle. Here are the kings." (At this point, he had my aunt Hilda close the fan

facedown. The kings are now on the bottom and the other four cards on top of the kings. Then he took the cards from Hilda and added them to the top of the deck facedown. This made me believe that the kings were on the top—but of course they began four cards down.)

"The rest of the deck represents the castle. One day Sabrina knocked on the door." (At this point, he knocked on the top of the cards.)

"The kings were all on the main floor of the castle by the door. Looking out the window, they panicked and cried, 'Oh, no! It's Sabrina!' Then they all scattered. The first and second kings went to the basement of the castle." (At this point, Hilda slid the top two cards off one at a time and, without showing them to me, slipped them into the middle of the deck.)

"The next two kings ran to the subbasement." (Hilda put the next two cards, one at a time, into the deck below where she had put the other two cards.)

"But Sabrina was impatient. She was a teenage witch. And she wanted to see the kings all at

once—and on the main floor. So she pointed her finger, and . . . *poof!*" (At this point, Salem hit the top of the deck with his paw.)

"And here are the kings, back on main floor of the castle with Sabrina." And there were the four kings!

Cool trick . . . for a cat.

What Card?

Salem is full of card tricks. But after I showed one to Harvey and Valerie, Harvey came up with this one:

Start with all the cards in the deck facedown, but leave the bottom card face up. Have a friend pick a card, and while he looks at it, you turn the deck over. Now all the cards are face up, but the card on top is facedown—and your friend still thinks all the other cards are facedown. (Remember she can only see the top card.) Then have your friend put his chosen card back in the pile. It will be facedown in the middle of the cards that are really face up! Distract your friend so you can turn over the cards again, so all of them are facedown. All you have to do to impress your friend is to search the deck for his card—the one that is face up. Be sure you don't let him see the last card, which is also face up.

Hey, even Salem didn't catch on to this one! Whoo-hoo!

Did I See That?

Sometimes I think I'm seeing things. Like the time I didn't want to watch lint falling with Salem. Then I realized how much fun it was. (Well, not really. I was having a really bad day, and it seemed like a very restful thing to do.)

But some tricks of the eye are really magical. They can fool us—or they can make us think. All right. You're right. Most of them just fool us.

Tricks of Light

Upstairs in our linen closet is the Other Realm, where my aunts, Salem, and I go to mingle with other witches and to see Drell, the head of the Witches' Council. Drell is all right, but he sometimes gets carried away with his spells—like the time he turned my friend Jenny into a grasshopper just because she was a mortal. It wasn't her fault that she ended up in the Other Realm while she was trying to find some towels in the linen closet.

Wait a sec . . . Drell's not the only one. My aunts are pretty good with a flash of light and a spell, too.

Here's one Aunt Zelda showed me: Get a flashlight, a plastic bottle (a one- or two-liter soda bottle works great), a long nail, and some newspapers. Fill the soda bottle completely with water and put the top back on tightly, making sure it doesn't leak. Lay the bottle on its side with the top hanging over a sink. Then turn

on the flashlight and aim it at the bottom of the soda bottle. Wrap the flashlight and half of the bottle with the newspaper (to keep the flashlight "hooked" to the bottle) with the flashlight pointed into the bottle, illuminating the contents. Next, holding the exposed part of the bottle over the sink, ask a parent to help you poke a hole in the side of the bottle with the nail. Then loosen the bottle cap to release the pressure, but not enough to let water out the top. Now put your finger under the water coming out of the nail hole in the bottle.

What you're noticing is not only water but also light on your finger!

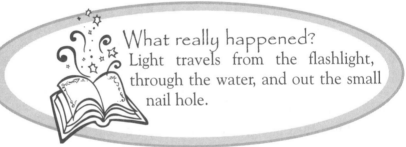

What really happened?
Light travels from the flashlight, through the water, and out the small nail hole.

What a Face!

I bought a picture for my aunts the other day. Aunt Hilda thought it was great, but Aunt Zelda just frowned at it. When I asked what was wrong, Aunt Hilda said it was the best drawing she'd ever seen of her twin cousins, Istan and Bull. Aunt Zelda didn't agree. She thought it looked like a glass vase she once saw being made in Austria a few centuries ago. Zelda thought Hilda was nuts. Hilda thought Zelda was nuts. Salem thought we were all nuts.

Take a look at this picture. What do you think?

There really is no right or wrong answer. This can be two faces or a vase. It's called an optical illusion. It's like the brain saying, "That's a face . . . No, wait a sec. That's a vase." In other words, the brain compares the picture to something it already knows and then makes a guess as to what it really is.

Big Watches

My aunts grew up in the fourteenth century, before television, phones, or CD players. That must have been rough. I'd hate to miss out on my favorite programs. They also told me they didn't wear watches, but you can bet they had sundials that used the sun and shadows to keep time. According to Aunt Hilda, the worst times were cloudy days and nighttime. They must have missed a lot of parties.

It is kind of cool to realize that you can tell time by the sun. My aunts helped me put a sundial together for a science project once. First, you have to know where north is, and the best way to find out is check a compass. Second, you have to know your latitude, and the best way to find that out is to check a world atlas. The atlas maps will usually show the general latitude of the place where you live. Take Boston, for example. It's at about 42 degrees latitude north of the equator; New Orleans, about

30 degrees latitude; Seattle, about 47 degrees.

Now cut a piece of heavy cardboard into two 6-by-9-inch pieces. Find a new pencil and sharpen it. Now gather a drawing compass, a protractor, a straight pin, a pen, some masking tape, and a ruler. Put one piece of the cardboard on a table with the long side up and down. Put the other piece of cardboard on top, then tape the two pieces together at the bottom (or shorter edge) like a hinge. Using the ruler, find and mark with the pen the point 5 inches from the bottom and 3 inches from either side of the top piece. Using the point of the compass as your center, draw a circle 5 inches in diameter.

Draw a line from the center, straight down to the bottom of the circle. Next, using the protractor, make a pencil mark every 15 degrees from the line on either side. All together, you should have five tick marks on either side of the line. To the left of the line, write in these numbers: 6-5-4-3-2-1 P.M. On the right side write in, 11, 10, 9, 8, 7, 6 A.M. Label the middle line 12.

Use the point of the straight pin to poke a hole in the center of the circle. Work the pencil point

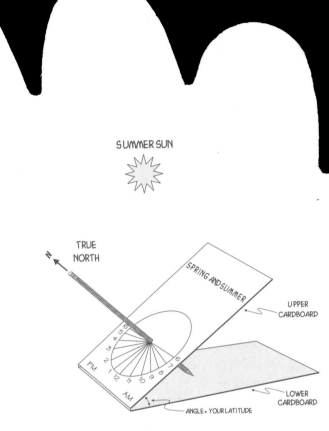

SUMMER SUN

TRUE NORTH

SPRING AND SUMMER

UPPER CARDBOARD

LOWER CARDBOARD

ANGLE = YOUR LATITUDE

PM 12 11 10 9 8 7 6 AM

through the cardboard, making sure to hold the pencil at a 90-degree angle to the cardboard. Move the cardboard up or down, making sure the angle between the upper cardboard (called the *gnomon*) and lower cardboard is the same degrees as your latitude.

Now take your sundial out on a sunny day and put it on a level surface. Point the gnomon to the north, and observe the dial. It should tell pretty close to the correct time.

I just love this kind of magic!

Which Way Is Witch?

Whenever I go back to school after summer vacation, I can easily get lost in the halls. Finding my classroom seems to take hours. That's when I could sure use Christopher Columbus—or a good compass—to guide me around.

Speaking of which, I know a way to make a quick compass so you know which way is north. You need a magnet, sewing needles, a chunk of Styrofoam (the peanuts that come in packages you get in the mail work great), and a bowl of water. All you have to do is rub one end of the needle on one end of the magnet a few times, to magnetize the needle. Next, break off a small chunk of the Styrofoam and push the needle through it until it comes out the other side. Put the needle in the water. It should float, and because you magnetized the needle, it should point north and south. To determine which end of the

needle is north, stand facing the direction the sun rises. That will be east, so north is to your left and south is to your right. Then label the north side of the Styrofoam with an N.

Whoo-hoo! Your own compass—and in less time than it takes for me to make a spell.

Toy Boat

I've skiied on Mars and done the limbo in the Other Realm, but I don't think I've ever sailed anywhere in the solar system except here on earth. I think it'd be neat—out in the sunshine and fresh air, depending on the planet. My two biggest problems would be deciding what bathing suit to wear and finding a life vest small enough to fit Salem!

 If you're not near a big sailing boat or a large body of water, there's a magic trick you can do with a smaller boat. You'll need a piece of heavy cardboard or light wood, scissors, a small piece of soap, and a bowl of water. Cut the cardboard or wood into the triangular shape of a boat, with the point at the front of the boat and the flat edge at the back. Cut a notch in the flat end. Fill the bowl with water, and put a small piece of soap in the notch at the back of the boat. Set the boat in the water—and watch it glide forward.

60

What really happened? This is like the pushing and pulling experiment we did, but in this case, the boat is bigger than the toothpicks. The soap weakens the water molecules at the surface, lowering the surface tension; and the boat is pulled forward by the stronger surface tension in the front. You couldn't use soap to move a big boat in the water. But this smaller version is still neat.

Magic Seal

No, this is not about a trained seal you see at an aquarium. This seal doesn't bark, and, unlike Salem, it doesn't even talk.

I accidentally discovered this experiment when I was doing the dishes the old-fashioned way—by hand, not in a dishwasher or with magic. All you need is a clean glass and a square piece of heavy cardboard or plastic. Fill the glass to the brim with water; then press the square of cardboard on top of the glass rim, making a good seal. Keeping the glass over the sink (sometimes it takes more than one try) and holding your hand over the cardboard, turn the glass over very carefully and then remove your hand from the cardboard. The lid stays in place and the water should stay inside the glass.

What really happened? Air is pressing on the cardboard with enough force to hold the cardboard in place. If you push down a corner of the cardboard and break the seal, the water will come splashing out.

Slurping up the Air

Air is definitely cool. (Or warm. And definitely necessary, since we have to breathe it.)

Speaking of air, mortals, witches, and cats are not the only ones who need it. Certain chemical reactions also need air—including a reaction we see very often: fire. Fire needs oxygen. No air means no fire. Try this quick experiment, *but only with adult supervision.*

Get a stable candle and a glass (*not plastic*) jar big enough to cover the candle. Ask an adult to help you light the candle. Now place the jar over the candle. If you wait for a few minutes, you'll see the flame die away—without anybody even blowing on it.

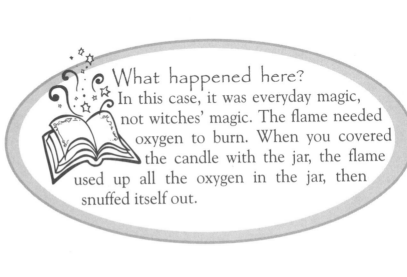

What happened here?

In this case, it was everyday magic, not witches' magic. The flame needed oxygen to burn. When you covered the candle with the jar, the flame used up all the oxygen in the jar, then snuffed itself out.

Bottle-Crushing Made Easy

What else can air do? Yes, folks, it can also crush a plastic bottle. Not that it's a such a great feat. My boyfriend, Harvey, can do that. Wait a sec . . . even Val and I can do that.

How about crushing the plastic bottle with no hands? Sure, my aunts can do that with a spell, and so can I. But air and heat can also do it—without hands or magic.

First, find a plastic container (a plastic milk jug works best) with a tight-fitting lid. Turn on the hot water in the sink and let it run until the water is pretty hot. Then rinse out the jug for about a half minute, empty the water out, and immediately screw on the cap. Set the empty jug in the refrigerator and let it sit for about three minutes. When you go back to the jug, it will have collapsed, almost as if magic had crushed it.

The reason is simple: the steam in the jug condenses (turns to liquid water) as it cools down. This decreases the pressure in the jug. Now the outside air pressure is greater than the inside air pressure—and the jug collapses.

Did I Hear That?

Not only do I sometimes see things, but I sometimes hear things, too. Most of the time it's just Salem trying to get my attention for a tummy rub. But sometimes there are the times when I wish I *had* heard something—like the date for my next trigonometry test. I thought I wrote it down, but I didn't. Anyway, here are some magical things about sounds that really make me listen.

67

Hum a Few Bars

When I hear certain funky tunes, I often feel like dancing. At other times I feel like singing along, because the music makes me feel so good. Even Salem's been known to swing his tail around, dancing to a good beat, but don't tell him I told you.

Do different types of music affect us in different ways? Scientists seem to think so, and the results are kind of magical. Certain types of music can stop some people from being sad, give them higher energy, and make them feel better about themselves. Other music helps people be more creative. And amazingly, some music can help people learn a foreign language faster.

So everyone likes different types of music. Some people like jazz, others like classical music or rock. Music makes them feel good.

Speaking of which, I think I'll go put on a CD.

Changing Your Tune

Now that I have my driver's license, I've been practicing driving the car, and my aunts and I have learned one valuable lesson: never let Salem drive a car. For one thing, he's too short. Also, he sheds all over the seats. And for another thing, he loves to beep the horn. He drives us crazy, so to speak.

The last time Salem tried to drive the car, I was standing on the front lawn. As he and Aunt Hilda flew by in the car, Salem beeped the horn—as usual. It was weird. As he was coming toward me, the horn sounded high-pitched, and as he went past me, the horn sounded lower in pitch. But it was still the same horn all the way.

After this happened, I checked it out with my old science teacher, Mr. Pool. He said it was an amazing science fact that was discovered more than a century ago—so Salem and my aunts probably knew the Austrian physicist who proved it.

His name was Christian Doppler, and the effect is called the Doppler effect.

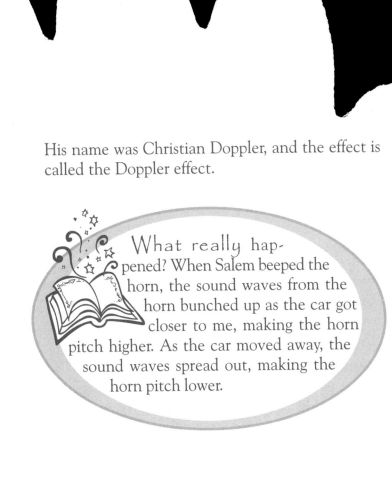

What really happened? When Salem beeped the horn, the sound waves from the horn bunched up as the car got closer to me, making the horn pitch higher. As the car moved away, the sound waves spread out, making the horn pitch lower.

Either way, Salem is *not* driving the car anymore. Too many hair balls!

Join the Band!

If you're like me, sometimes you dream about being in a rock band. Now, what would I play? Maybe the guitar? Or beating on the drums? Of course, I *could* be the singer. Even for a witch, it's hard to decide what to do!

So I thought I'd try them all. I tried singing, but Salem started howling. Next, I tried the drums, but my aunts said I needed to practice keeping the rhythm. I needed another instrument, so I grabbed my *Discovery of Magic* book, called up the Index Man, and said, "Music, man!"

Here is what the Index Man found: How to make a guitar—and you can make one, too. Let me read some of this to you:

 You'll need four or five rubber bands of various lengths and thicknesses, a tissue box with an oval hole in the top, two pieces of wood about half an inch thick and as wide as the

box. Stretch the rubber bands lengthwise over the box, keeping them about a half an inch apart. Then work the pieces of wood under the rubber bands on either end of the box. This holds up the bands so they won't touch the box, like the bridge of guitar.

Here's the magic! By strumming the bands, you can make sounds. And you can change the high or low pitch of the notes by making some bands looser and other bands tighter. Just keep experimenting with the bands until you can play a simple tune.

Look out, world—here I come!

Bottle-Music Magic

I've been trying to persuade my aunts to join me with my hand-made guitar. You know, maybe start our own magic band. But they didn't like the name I chose for the band: Sabrina and the Aunts. (Their loss.)

Of course my aunts didn't know what instruments they wanted to play. I checked with the Index Man again, and he suggested they try clarinets, oboes, trumpets, or trombones. Different shapes of wood and metal can produce many amazingly different sounds when you blow into them—like pipes. Here are some pipes you can make:

Gather five empty glass bottles of the same size. Fill one bottle with water almost to the top. Fill the second about three-fourths full, the third half full, and the fourth a quarter full. Leave the last bottle empty. Now

blow across the top of each bottle—and listen to the notes. For a slightly different sound, you can tap gently on each bottle with a spoon to produce the notes.

What really happened? Every time you blow across the top of the bottle, the air inside the bottle vibrates. When you blow across a bottle with less air and more water, you get a high-pitched sound. Blowing across a bottle with more air and less water will give you a low-pitched sound. You can change the pitch by raising or lowering the level of the water.

Now all my aunts and I have to do is get our act together!

Out of the House

What's outside? The sun is shining, the birds are singing, and . . . well, if you can get past the talking trees, it's magical to be outside.

My favorite thing about the out-of-doors is the plants.

See if you don't agree with me that they're kind of magical!

Sweating Plants?

Did you ever see a plant sweat? Try this magic.

 Place a clear plastic bag over the leaves and stem of a plant (you can use a houseplant for this, too), tying it tight around the stem near the soil. Be sure none of the plant touches the bag, except where it's tied to the stem near the soil line. Set the plant in the sun, and leave it there for a few hours.

Yikes! The plant is sweating!

You and I sweat when we exercise, but this plant was standing still. Certainly it can't really be sweating?

What really happened? This plant is not sweating. It's called transpiration, a big word that means the plant is releasing water into the air, as part of the earth's natural water cycle.

In fact, some big trees lose gallons of water every day to transpiration.

So take the plastic bag off the plant, and let it continue to do its magic!

Magic in the Dark

My two aunts, Salem, and I often hang out in the second-floor linen closet. That's how we get to the Other Realm and visit the Witches' Council. We don't bother with the other closets. They're just too dark. But there is some plant magic you can do in the dark of a closet.

 You will need some seeds (larger seeds, such as beans, work well), several paper towels, and a cookie sheet or a large piece of aluminum foil. Dampen the paper towels and spread them out on the cookie sheet. Then place several seeds on the wet paper towels. Cover the seeds with more wet paper towels. Place the cookie sheet in a dark closet, and check each day to make sure the towels are still wet. (You can sprinkle them with more water, enough to keep them wet but not sopping wet.) After a week or less, most seeds will pop right open.

The seeds swell with water, and some seeds may even grow hairy-looking sprouts. If you plant these sprouts in the soil, they should grow without a problem.

Mini-Beanstalk

I already admitted that I skimped on the magic jumping beans recipe I tried once, and when the beans made it to the backyard, they grew into the biggest beanstalk you ever saw. I've been thinking of using the same recipe to grow the biggest tomato ever—one that will keep the household in spaghetti sauce for years! Reality check: I forgot *how* I skimped on the recipe.

That's no problem. I still like the smaller plants. They're amazing. Just watch how they grow. It seems like magic to watch a plant grow from a tiny seed to something like a carrot.

And of course, plants are run by the sun. Plants like the sun, and need the sun, as do people.

 You will need a couple of seeds (the large bean seeds work best), a short glass jar filled with dirt, and a shoebox or some other box that has a lid. Place one or two seeds in the soil and water

them every other day until the seeds starts growing (how fast they grow will depend on the type of seed). Cut a 1 ½-inch hole in either side of the box. Place the jar with the growing seeds in the box, on the side opposite the hole and put the lid back on. Put the box in a sunny place so the sunlight shines in the hole. Keep watering the plant every other day—and at the same time, watch how the plant sprout grows toward the light.

I know what happens here—I read it in my science book. Like a moth that heads for light at night, the plant heads in the direction of the sunlight. It needs the light's energy to make its own food, just as humans need to eat to grow.

Color Me Blue or Red?

Harvey, my boyfriend, invited me to a formal dance last week. He wanted to wear a small flower in the lapel of his tux. He chose a white flower, and I wanted him to wear a blue . . . no, I mean a red one.

Uh-oh! The dance was getting closer and I couldn't decide.

Do you want to know what I did? No, I didn't flash my finger at the flower and change the color. I performed a bit of natural magic—something you can try, too.

 You'll need a white carnation with a long stem, some food coloring (such as blue and red), a pair of scissors, two glasses, and one cup of fresh tap water. Have an adult help you slice the stem of the flower in half lengthwise about halfway up toward the flower. Pour a half cup of the water into each of the two glasses. Now

add enough food coloring to each glass of water to make one a deep blue and the other a deep red. Put one end of the flower stem in the blue water and the other into the red water, and leave it that way for about forty-eight hours. Ta-dah! It's a half-and-half flower!

What really happened? The colored water traveled up little tubes in the stem called *xylems*, and the colored water turned the flower half blue and half red. That's how plants get minerals from the soil, too.

The red-and-blue flower I gave Harvey was the hit of the dance!

Pressing Petals

I'm always forgetting to get cards for people's birthdays. I know I can whip one up using my magic, but sometimes I like to make the card myself. It's fun: I get to collect flowers and make up poems for my friends. Like my recent card to Salem. It read, "Roses are red, violets are pink, just be happy you weren't turned into a mink." (Hey, *I* thought it was cute.)

 You can magically create some cards, too. You'll need some heavy paper for the notecards, some wild or garden flowers small enough to fit on the card, paper towels, and glue or cellophane tape. Lay the flowers on top of two layers of paper towels, carefully making sure the flower petals and leaves lie flat. Cover the flowers with two more paper towels and place a heavy book (a thick telephone book or dictionary will work) on top. Let the flowers dry for at least

several days, and if you live in a rainy place, let them dry for a week. They'll be dry and stiff because the heavy book and paper towels squeezed the water out of the flowers.

Glue or tape the dried flowers to the front of the card. Use your imagination—you can make bookmarks, gift tags, or decorated boxes with your dried flowers, too.

Getting the Green Out

I absentmindedly left a potted plant on the grass a few days ago to give it some sunshine. When I remembered it, I ran outside and picked up the pot. I noticed something strange about the grass: it looked as if I had just painted the grass underneath the pot with a light green paint. (Nice color, but I doubt my aunts would want me to repaint the entire front lawn to match!)

What happened? Just a bit of plant magic. You can try this on a corner of your own lawn, but make sure it's a spot that your parents approve of first. For this, all you need is a garbage can lid or a clay pot that usually holds plants. Put the lid or the pot over a patch of green grass and leave it there for seven days. Lift up the lid or pot after a week, and what has happened?

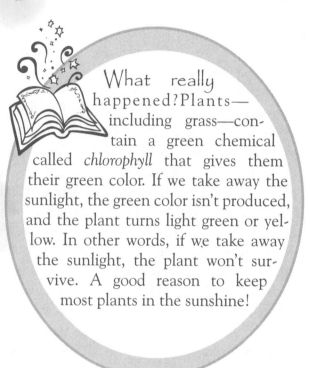

What really happened? Plants— including grass—contain a green chemical called *chlorophyll* that gives them their green color. If we take away the sunlight, the green color isn't produced, and the plant turns light green or yellow. In other words, if we take away the sunlight, the plant won't survive. A good reason to keep most plants in the sunshine!

All right. We've definitely seen some pretty neat stuff in the form of everyday magic. You've probably also noticed that not everything has to be conjured up by pointing a finger. Sure, I do magic in that way, but I'm even more astonished at the magic that surrounds us in everything we see, touch, taste, hear, and smell.

While you were having fun with the magical activities, you no doubt thought of some of your own. And you didn't even need to borrow Aunt Zelda's lab-top chemistry set or visit the Other Realm! Don't stop here. Go ahead. Look around some more. Ask questions. And write down other magical things you see—sort of your own magical handbook. See if you can continue to amaze your friends, and yourself, with all the other magical things you find.

Have fun!

— Sabrina

About the Author

In her youth Patricia Barnes-Svarney was usually found tinkering with typewriters and toasters or mixing the wrong chemicals from her chemistry set—which often toasted the garage. Now she is usually found writing nonfiction science books and science-fiction novels and articles, a seemingly safer occupation. Her fiction credits include books from the series *The Secret World of Alex Mack, Star Trek: Starfleet Academy,* and *Salem's Tails,* all for young readers. Her hobbies are hiking, herb gardening, rock hunting, and birding. She lives in Endwell, New York, with her husband. She also tends to sundry squirrels, chipmunks, birds, and the occasional rabbit.